EROTIKON

EROTIKON

Poems

Susan Mitchell

HarperCollins*Publishers*

Grateful acknowledgment is made to the editors of the following publications in which these poems first appeared:

Atlantic Monthly: "Golden Bough: The Feather Palm"
Fence: "The Grove at Nemi"
New Republic: "Golden Bough"
Paris Review: "Autobiography," "Girl Tearing Up Her Face," and "Venice"
Ploughshares: "Pussy Willow (An Apology)" and "Wind/Breath,
   Breath/Wind"
Yale Review: Sections 1–3 of "Bird: A Memoir"

"Girl Tearing Up Her Face" was collected in *Best American Poetry 1996.*
"Venice" was included in *Ecstatic Occasions, Expedient Forms,* edited by
   David Lehman (University of Michigan Press, 1996).

HarperCollins books may be purchased for educational, business, or sales promotional use. For information please write: Special Markets Department, HarperCollins Publishers Inc., 10 East 53rd Street, New York, NY 10022.

FIRST EDITION
Designed by Sam Potts
Printed on acid-free paper

Library of Congress Cataloging-in-Publication Data

Mitchell, Susan.
   Erotikon: poems/by Susan Mitchell.—1st ed.
      p.   cm.
   ISBN 0-06-055353-7
   I. Title.
PS3563.I824E76   2000
811.'54 — dc21   99-16853

00 01 02 03 04 ❖ HC 10 9 8 7 6 5 4 3 2 1

CONTENTS

Acknowledgments   vii

ONE

Bird: A Memoir   3

TWO

Pussy Willow (An Apology)   19

Wind/Breath, Breath/Wind   22

Girl Tearing Up Her Face   26

Golden Bough: The Feather Palm   30

Autobiography   32

Venice   35

Golden Bough   38

The Grove at Nemi   40

THREE

Erotikon   45

FOUR

Golden Fleece   73

Notes   75

ACKNOWLEDGMENTS

I am grateful to the Guggenheim Foundation and the Lannan Foundation for fellowships and to Claremont University for the Kingsley Tufts Poetry Award: The generous support of all three made these poems possible. Special thanks must also go to Robert Jones, my editor at HarperCollins and my friend, for his faith in this book: His sensitive listening and his presence at several of my readings nurtured some of these poems in their earliest stages. And heartfelt thanks must also go to my copy editor, Sue Llewellyn, a connoisseur of stylistic nuances with an uncanny ear and perfect pitch.

ONE

Bird: A Memoir

If you go back far enough in my family tree there are birds.
Tall, hunched-up proud birds and also small skittery birds
that move like shadows in the branches. How do I know this?
Is it something about the face that looks back at me
from mirrors? Something in the way I move? In my voice?
Yes, it's true I can mimic their songs, but only
if I sip warm water first.

Take, for example, the question of locus, blithe recitatives
of space where perch I. Or flying, stutter forth on
equilibriums of song. Into the vacant, into the empty
and open, I hesitant, groping, not at all daring, cowardly
and even whimpering put myself deliberately. Why? Why
savor the precarious, the unsteady from which in all
directions I look out?

Wimble and wight, a phrase I like to repeat. Is it
to calm myself? I am not adverse to fluffs of comfort,
and have been known to myself to sing *Bye Baby Bunting.*
And in a voice playful, intimate, haven't I pounced
on myself with *snug as a bug in a rug? Wimble and wight,*
perhaps more of a tonic, flagellum or flageolet,
with which I whip myself to glees of teeter.

Blue with some straws growing out of it, blue with reedy spires
sticking up, with scrannel and scratch. For what am I
heartsick? For what yearn I, undaunted by blooms upgathered?
Without nets, without catches and clutches,
I throw myself into the wild waste places;

I what heaves me into preens of anguish and delight. And for what,
this prayer upward into sweep and bough?

Of my childhood this remains. A casino by the sea. Inordinate
desire. How I loved to stuff myself with the unripe,
the unready, the rough and ragged greens of undigested thought.
And these ancestral lurkings in my face, only their movements
visible, as if something had withdrawn deeper in, closed off
by leaves, branches—a weight removing itself, unbalancing
into trill and quaver.

Bricoleur is what I am. Collector of scraps: sappy, juicy,
unraveling, precipitous. Fragments I yearn together
to build what? A tisket? A tasket? No, I am not one
to nest, not one for whom the tucked-in, the tiggy, tiggy
touchwood matters overmuch. Not for me the serial
order of ducks floating their flotillas
of domestic bliss for all to see.

More for me, the branch detached, disconnected, where I,
forswonk, forswatt, into accolades of space swing out.
Not for nothing, I tell myself, *snug* rhymes with *smug.*
Of dizziness I make my *locus amoenus.* Upladder and down.
Of dizziness, my *locus ille locorum.* Oh, place of places.
So what if rungs are missing. Still rings out what unquiets
me most. How close are terror and pleasure.

— • —

But perhaps of my loves it is necessary to say something.
Those I supped with, those with whom riotously I danced
or in games of hide and seek played for weeks on end
in brief forepleasures of song. In love I was never hesitant.
Never coy. To savor, however unsavory, I *avis sapiens,*
sometimes rash, foolhardy even, rushed forward, fipple
to bowstring, giddy with galore.

How to apportion the self from branch to branch? *To taste*
and by tasting know. To delight to alight. These were
the mottoes of my youth. And also, *song rejoices*
the mouth. And where buds in goose bumps all along
the branch, where newness in flummery foiled and fooled,
I the manifold its many folds unfolding filled full of,
always ready with my *buon appetito.*

O Tite, tute, tati, tibi, tanta, tyranne, tulisti! The kisses
tumbling over one another like the letters of a tongue twister.
How I love a branch rucked and jammed with buds, with leaf
and flower spurred. How I love those difficult passages
for recorder and flute, the stops so close together, the mouth
crouched awkward, backward bent, all upside down to play.
So I, fractious, by fractions advanced each day.

Whistles that blow out feather tongues to tease and tickle.
So much between the self and others is maunder and mumble.
So much is hem and haw, quaver and falsetto. Thus began
my *Erotikon*—thus, my book of books, round-robin encyclical,

round-the-head and round-the-corner, memorabilia
of mobs and rabble, corraling coral with carols, honeycomb
and wasp's nest, columns of hum and humble.

On holidays, oriflamme and banderole. Spills of ribbon.
But especially balls of bright paper, yellow wound
around green, green around pink, pink around white. Faster
and faster, I unwound each band, though I knew: in the end,
only ribbons of paper to twirl and dizzy in. Who would give
a gift made entirely of opening? For my third investigation
I shall write about sleep. For my seventh, laughter.

Am I waiting for something extraordinary to happen?
A sign? An adventure? A leaf that twists oddly as it falls?
Sometimes extraordinary things happen in sleep.
In sleep Criseyde dreamed a bird exchanged its heart
with hers, tearing under her breast with its eagle claws.
Chaucer wrote this, adding moonlight and feathers
white as bone. *Nothyng smerte,* he said: she felt no pain.

What cages me? What in this wide hugey plain of language
is not mine to spit and spew? What sounds me
through bars of patois, creoles of my past and future lives?
And what did that story mean? Love makes us other
than human? Rapacious birds of prey? Hybrid creatures?
I have looked into a bird's eye (bright, yellow, mineral)
no crumb of speech could feed.

— • —

Sheen on which the breath fogs up, clears, fogs again.
Crepuscular scatterings, great solifluctions.
Husky, the notes catching on each other, slurring. The cry
coming apart as it descends icily. Why do I want to take
this into my throat? After it comes an echo,
ghost scream, a specter. Making my throat a shaft
through which what?

Music, I could understand that need. But this cry through
which the hawk funnels itself. This narrow, this pinched—
what if all I had were two-line stanzas? But a scream
is not language, not of any language part. The same scream
over and over, whipping me, lashing. The way sexual
desire is always the same feeling, the same channel
opening up between the legs, clawing

the body, finding the weakest spot to break out of.
Tearing the body apart just to get out.
To open its mouth onto the other.
To suck lips, other lips, into itself.
And biting, biting, biting.
Knowing in advance, this is how it's going to be. And yet,
surprised, always the same surprise.

Have I misled you? Did you think memoir meant some chronicle
of a great or splendid or tumultuous or even hysterical
century in which the famous lived? Did you expect the tone
and hue of the heroic? Some pilgrim's progress? Some
summa, some summing-up? What, anyway, is a life? Why not

a memoir of the never finished, the only partly done? Or,
the not said, the not sung? The underdrill of trill?

Sometimes I think this, our life on earth, is an egg
to break out of. I am claustrophobic. Into the next, into
the come-after and come-what-may I shall peck and peck
myself, all naked of language, with only my meter
to sound the way. What is it I am starved for?
Eternity? Infinity? Forever? Or some
other word for emptiness?

To which, hush. I stillness for stillness give, I silence
for silence. If I am built around something I can never
understand, must I its keeper be? Must I caretake
the indigestible? The secrets that interest me
are those from myself I keep, holes in which I lurk
by me undetected, so smoothly I the depth
of shadow mix and match.

Heavenly perfume one body takes from another. Song
sung without opening the mouth. Confession is not
the same as intimacy. And language does not open
the territory. More like a bird calling, always up ahead,
yearning me deeper in. Here is a riddle for you,
unheimlicher bird. What is so strange
it feels like home? It calls. I follow.

— • —

Today I am perched on the tip of my tongue. Which of my
seven heavens shall I fly to? Today my attention
is everywhere at once. To disperse, to unfocus
into showers of gold and tinsel is my one desire.
Why must everything be dragged through intellect?
I am sick of meaning. Today I shall throw myself away
in puff after puff of furbish and spangle.

There was a garden: at night they snuffed the flowers,
but not their smells. Lemons burned in the trees.
A place for love? Or a place for work? I can
no longer tell the two apart.
When the wind blew there was the sound of a sea.
My favorite moments flew off like spray.
What did I learn from this?

I liked to sleep there and also read. Was I content?
I liked to copy out of books words
that pleased me, sometimes whole passages, and as I
did this, there would rise up inside me
like a wave, there would start in my chest and
push up to my throat, a stairway without
any destination, ascending me again and again.

Does joy have a purpose? From Plautus I copied out
a single word, *ciccus,* core of the pomegranate,
that elusive fruit which escapes the eater
every bite of the way. Surely there is more to it
than this, I'd think, sucking at seeds.

Surely when I get to the center, the core: but the core
is throwaway, and *ciccus* also means *worthless*.

Can anything said or thought be taken back?
Today in my *Erotikon* I wrote, *Art is relentless, it*
refuses to look away. It stares into me
with its hard mineral eye, inhuman.
Once of myself I caught a look
all unaware in a mirror: a me apart
from any idea I have of me.

What a terrifying thing it is to be alone
with another. Should I have followed? That glimpse
lasted a moment, no more—an acrobat, it leaped
into a world more daring: I was trapezed,
flared open, as when a cellist
drags the bow unendurably across the strings, and a more
than ordinary grieving—reckless, unheeding—begins.

Should I have gone there? In my *Erotikon*
I always hope to find some shock
of music never listened to by me. Should I have
entered before it closed? It was all so quick, like
birds shifting from branch to branch.
And would it have included love?
Or does love need a world of its own?

— • —

Bright béchamels, huge honeycombs
of splash and frazil. Why make and remake
in heptagon and heptaglot,
in heptarch and heptateuch, those places
dear to my heart? Still hidden, still
undisclosed by me, deep
pools of marsh where in winter the ice, uneven in

yodels of foam; doilies frothing
the mouth of a dog; thick, creamy dribblings
crusted over; epicures of drool murmured
to a standstill. But why seven? you ask. Why
seven days to the week? Or seven
ages of man? Why seven against Thebes, seven
wise men, and seven swans afloating?

And why did Persephone eat seven
seeds of the pomegranate? Why not five? Or nine?
Seven makes half a sonnet and a royal rhyme.
If Noah had sent me instead
of the dove, if he had thrown me into the air
like a handful of seeds, would I
have come back with seven of everything?

Seven rivers (two polluted, five clear and brimming)?
Seven mountains (three with sides dug out
for gravel pits, the other four still smoking)?
Fetishist is what I am, and seven's
my shoe, my Cinderella. After a long day's work

it's lists I retire to: what Montezuma
sent as tribute to Cortés, what

the good ship *Marie de Wilshore* carried
in her hold, what was served
at the funeral of the Duchess of Lancaster in 1374:
comfits of aniseed, gillyflower, gobbet royal.
The crowd was always my element, the huddle comprehensive,
plenum and quorum feasting in flight; the crowd
was always my joy, hordes fleeting

and contingent, coveys of fireflies, chariots
of finches; charmed, I dally, lagging
behind the names of hosts, heaps, assemblies.
On telephone wires, in malls, in the sky where great
muddy puddles, where sloughs and muckholes, birds
uproarious and ordinary, gather; on roofs
slanted and pinnacled, on topmost

branches, on ledges and edges, on spikes, entire
populations back and forth
shifting their stycchic, their stanzaic
repetitions, commotion from bird to bird passed on
generation to generation (*remember this*),
continuousness without anchor wheeling (*remember*), immensity
through their purposeless buildings soaring in.

— • —

What is desire a cure for? And if so, can I ever have
enough appetites to stuff myself with, all my mouths
transported to health with a single bite? Of all desires
song goes farthest. But how is it I have forgotten
the sea, forgotten its conglutinations to enumerate?
Its congelations and water dripping from the roofs of caverns,
its brave coagulations of salt to honor?

I have been to its edges where it rocks and cradles, where
hisses and vast exhalations solemnly and with abandon—
its seepages and propagations witnessed. And as a child
stood before it—I, like a precipice, a vast yearning,
a without to equal the birds calling in their infinite
combinations: curlew and sandpiper, whimbrel
and whillet, and forget not the gull, blacktailed, glaucous.

What must I know to say what I know? Listening
is a risky business, terrifying as flowers opening in spring
their vulnerable (*voluptuous,* I almost said) petals, though
the first flowers are like swords, and I their gladiator fallen.
Am I a gifted listener? Despite dangers, picking from the surface
this sound, then that, where the current foams up
in urinous chords its acrimonious secretions.

To attend. To hear in *attention* the tension—and a tone
tentative at first, but with listening, tonic. To be stretched
on tenterhooks of aural surge. Not to miss out on anything:
to make that my lifework. The ear excited for longer
and longer until listening, breathless, cries out.

Or, on a dare, slipping in and out of meaning, and in the wild
screams of loss, filled full. Is that fulfillment?

What would it have been like to live before the dictionary,
before words in columns, the rank and file assembled?
What would it have been like to nest in a language
untamed, unfixed, even my name wobbling, its letters
never the same? In the unanchored to build, in drifting
to weave and waver? In its rushes to live unafraid
of the motion in emotion or the ocean in commotion?

To perch—or to percolate? Oh, I am restless as dice.
Does this make me a bad omen? But see, like the seasons,
like cloud, I am changing. From grumpy to grumous.
First dowdy, then doughty, then doughy. No, I was never
one of your carved and painted, never one of your precise
as a Swiss watch in its little weskit of birdy black and gray.
Never one of your *nose nappy, tae titly, moo merry.*

*Oh, there were two birds sat on a stone. One flew away
then there was one.* No, I was never one you could fix
on the jacket of a book: in its black-and-white photo
forever young. And if to myself I say, *Knock, knock!*
and then, feigning surprise, *Who's there?* Do birds give
themselves names, syllables undetected of light and plunge,
which those untutored fail to catch on rill and rim?

— • —

Perhaps it's true, my happiest moments are the anticipation
of other moments still to come. The evening, yet to be
unfurled, but its aroma released, burdening
the air with the heavy breathing
of the trees, their panting louder than the sky,
which has just let out squeals of acetylene and orange.
A smell so throaty, so from the armpits of the trees.

Oh, to be fragrant, to break open into a great
fury of smells. Is aroma physical? Or of the spirit?
That promise of spirit tasting frustrates?
What the mouth can never close on,
twang of the elusive where instinct blurs
to indistinct? What I hunger for
is not a parable of anything.

Like feelings I come and go. Like those puddles birds
drink from after a heavy rain. Gone by morning.
And if the incomprehensible is all
that's left of self, the personal, the private? An outlying
beyond the sludge and gas stations, beyond
the medians where the music trembles
into blare and shouting.

Bird be nimble, bird be quick, or the small
plot you call your bower will grow
into a long boring story. There is a feeling that
comes before migration, a hastening, an upward
rush into the lining of something luxurious

no one has ever worn.
Is this the future—

sound not yet an imitation
of anything? *Pekke hem right up!* a voice
commanded in a dream. Peck up *what?*
The swirling dust, the unclear? Nightly didder of birds
when syllables intimate—but time is short.
From now on I will listen only to the arias.
Spare me the long slow walk of recitative.

Do you become what you listen to? Branch
dipping, little gustos of fear, sudsy
places in the music, steepnesses, caliginous tropes?
My favorite songs are like thirst
as it is quenched. And oh, that pale aching
green of twigs when the bark
is stripped back.

Sometimes at dusk another voice begins, overripe
sweet to spoiling, a green beyond green.
So much comes at the last moment.
Like the final dance of the evening with its underbreath
of promise, its twinges of titillation, the tango
extending nervously its shadows, the long legs
of desire striding toward faster and faster tempos.

TWO

Pussy Willow (An Apology)

Why delay? Today I stopped
to rub the fur, like the tender
ear of a cat, stopped

to stroke the lush gray
plush (and oh, the pink! as if
the cat had rasped

itself to frenzy, to an
ecstasy of itch
all raw

this steak tartare, this
chafe of meat) and
because of this

I was late (the willows in
their bins outside
the florist almost as tall as I)

and once again, have traded
friendship for
dillydally.

I had to take off
my gloves, and I would have
taken off my skin

(for why should I put
a barrier between
myself and anything?)

to pluck, to blow back
each separate tuft
of foam (in down, sink down)

because I cannot keep my hands
off the world and the world
out of my breath. What

does the world want (anyway)
of me with its pussy willows, with
its tears and angers

its greeds and splendors, its
petitions of
skyscrapers and waterfalls?

And what do I want with
its famous and forgotten? And is
this the purpose of my life,

to figure this out? Or is it
to touch and be touched? And if
I love the world more than

any one person, or if I love
one person more
than the world, what

does this say of me?
And what do I say to friends
when they keep me waiting,

Oh, dally, friend, delight
so that I may rub
it from your body

its furs and gewgaws, its
horrors and sweetnesses, so you may
deliver it to me, you

the messenger, the unwinged,
the prosaic in all
its scratch and bliss?

Wind/Breath, Breath/Wind

But later, to teach myself humility, I worked
exclusively with breath, with the insubstantial, with what
does not last, not leave a record behind

those streamers, those ribbons we trail from our bodies

banners, flags of the living,

excrement of the mouth and lungs, though we
do not like to think

the spirit is the waste of the body. Oh yes, I started
with something grand as wind and when I said
wind, slowly tasting the whine in the word

I could hear the high-pitched plaintive cry
of a dog intoxicated with grief,

the whip and whinny working itself up to new heights. Up there,

the wind is graspable, a shaft, a pole, a tree nothing can
topple, nothing uproot the wind
by its own hair, except the wind.

Once upon a time, the winds had names. But you know that.
Aeolus. Boreas. Zephyrus. Now they are anonymous
as crowds in a subway.

I am part of the great leftover, the way dragonflies
are part of what moves, the male pushing
into the female, the wind
pushing him pushing into her, how it blows
through them with an excitement different from their own,

the rush through the nostrils audible
as the start of an alphabet, that place where the singer gasps,
her breath forcing the music wider, now it

has to include the body, its limps and stutters.

I wanted something we all had in common, a material
ordinary as air, inexpensive, easily available—

there must be as many breaths as brushstrokes, some thick
and impastoed, others phlegmy or drooling spit.

How useless the saw and drill, how useless to think of patina,
the shine water takes, the gleam of ice. Air takes
no shine, is passed through the mouth

where animals are chewed up and blood, where semen and saliva
where kisses and the tongue sucked in and out, throbbing.

Sometimes I think there are two people breathing
inside me, one running in terror
at last gasp, the other in hot pursuit, a killer, a maniac.

I am the hysteric caught in between, I hold them
here in my chest where they begin
to warm and take on the shape of my ribs, they leave

their mark in me, the way a boat leaves an impression
in the wet sand, and even after the boat
breaks up and falls to pieces,
its stain, its shadow like an X ray I feel inside me, it passes

now from my mouth to your ear, my tongue ungluing
each whorl, each labyrinthine, though
we are not lovers, and isn't it strange when we take the air

into our mouths, it is renamed *breath,* and the fact
that we can change air into breath, and breath
back into air, is what proves

we are alive, the muscles of the breath
which are the movers, all covered with a thick network
of sinews, and some breaths are like strong

swimmers swimming one inside the other, passing
through narrow portals, and the way

the glassmaker's breath bubbles into the glass
an effervescence, intoxication
of the diver, the molten pulled by lips and forceps—

or do I mean the breath?—how the body keeps giving it away,
profligate, the ease of it, the uncaring.

Girl Tearing Up Her Face

Where it's rubbed out, start there, where it's torn,
where something like a burn in cloth, the hot
metal pressed too long, forgotten

                              in paper the worm-
hole, the eaten up, the petal frayed, browning
at the edges, the flower's
flesh like cigarette paper

consumed by the breath sucked back into
the body: yes, body, that's what
that is what—no, I'm not stalling, body

is what I mean to talk about, what I have
on my mind, in my mind, my mind
in the body of the body—

and what's disturbing, yes, that above all: the joy
right there in her face, the girl's, as if she
had been smacked with it, the big fish joy,

a cold hard wet smack by something flailing out, this
joy thing throwing itself around

or as if someone had thrown a pudding, a thick batter
and now her face was trying to work its way
through that mess—yes, joy, the mess,

the ugliness of it because it has not yet
been practiced, the mouth trying out
positions before the mirror, the mouth

performing little sounds up and down the scale
of pleasure—the joy not yet prepared
for anyone else to look at—the shock like

a flashbulb going off, a camera
pouncing before one is ready, before
one has run the tongue over, taken a bite

out of the smile, hands arranging the hair.
The girl looks all doors open, the sheer
weight of her coming starting

to come and her body sucking it back,
inhaling each tooth of bliss,
running her fingers up and down the comb:

it's that ugly I want to rub my face in, that
blossoming, as if a tree had suddenly—
the stamen pushing up out of

the petals, the throat of the apple, its
woods and the dark seeds
bursting the blossom, so I push

her back, I open her mouth right there
where she sits on the swing,
a rage of delight shivering the tree's—

can I say *flesh,* can I say *skin?*—and
I can't bear to look at her
doing that, it seems too private, as if she

had been caught having a dream she
didn't know she was having,
all her wings run over by pleasure, joy

having a tantrum all over her, this
limp rag of beaten-down, and the photographer
thinking, Yeah, this is it, the moment

he wants to last and last—the forever: now with
the girl falling asleep on the swing,
her sleep in full view, its lids

pulled open so the deep anesthesia
of her pleasure is suddenly visible, sucked
inside out so he can hear every sound

a face can make, and it's those sounds
he wants to shudder down on, those
cries with the flesh still

attached, and what they have
been pulled from gaping and
ragged and this is what will be handed

to the girl in black and white, this face
that in two seconds would have
changed and gone on changing, this face

she never suspected, and of course, she'll have to
rip it into pieces and keep ripping
because even now I can't bear

to look at her suddenly awake, I want
her asleep again, unbegun, unstarted, the shades
drawn so I can float every which possible, all

manner of across her face accommodating
as a lap, and I don't think,
For God's sake, she's only eleven, what does she

know or understand of anything? I'm—I'm flooding
even as she rips herself in two, even as
she vows never to be this person

I'm putting my head down in her lap, pushing
her back on the swing with so much force—
What could split open? What could eat her up?

Golden Bough: The Feather Palm

as if as if as if a hiss a swish of
fake of fraud fraudulent
among the genuine
but why green should be genuine and this other
this bleached this platinum this gold
oh, I can be plain I can be
plain green in the slippery sunlight the oily—
like an extra limb like a fetish
attached to the tree *Cocos plumosa,* the feather
palm, queen of queens, like a fetish
a golden dildo the la-di-la
flies and wasps and bees smear their
mouths and eyes with spangled with vulgar
with not at all good taste like those beaded
curtains hung up as room dividers:
from a distance peroxide and honey, up loud
a xanthous a luteolous a gilded auric
screech, who said the past
was chaste was not this cheap
aroma that whooshes from the flowers
bunched in fascicles, each
petaled gold rolled in bundles
but already starting to
brown at the bend and flank
where the hum the drone the whir:
what smell
holds them there sucking by mouth
fastening and lapping
bits of gold bits of garish

as if the branch
like a breast flowing its slow gaudy flow
and all the bees with their laughing gear
pushed out ready to diddle
the dingle-dangle the ding-dong the dingus,
and wouldn't I
for days on end like the flies
mucked with gold guzzling
fumbling the golden lather the plush
swaying back and forth, to
be lifted like an aroma

Autobiography

Who am I who speaks to you?

Though that's not it exactly. Try this. What behind
the eyes had looked out so central, so
solid, was no longer
in its saccharins, its careful
modulations, not even

a shadow of its . . . For a long time I watched

the unbraiding into thinner and thinnest . . . like clouds or
tall stalks of something in a field through which wind,
the tassles untasseling . . .

I was behind where I stood and up ahead looking back.

Though that's not it exactly.

How did I feel about all this? I said
that is not the question most likely
to succeed, but even so I'll take it the way

male and female are conveniences, rough categories, the make-do.

Is precision a better way? As soon as they asked me
which was more enjoyable, I lost the taste
of myself. Though to call who I am
Tiresias would limit
the story. It was as if the one talking

were now a handful of crystals
absorbing the rays of the sun, a spectrum
out there in space, all the colors of the rainbow
primal and urgent, tensed, arched over,

and also looking down into a stream
where flowed and wavered the reds, the yellows, green.

I don't want to get lost in explaining. The colors
were doing what I was, a correlative
for anger, joy, fear, wonder, eagerness and more, all

the emotions so I could look at them, taking my time,
naming each one. And that was it, folks.

Think flicker and fluid and flow, and all of it
seething and reaching out for
attention the way serpents coupling and uncoupling and

no particular reason why one at any given moment
reigns supreme, all of it up
for grabs, so to speak.

No, there was no enclosure, no frame.

I was placed in understanding. And from looking

so long inside, as if at the sun, I was
blinded and had to grope at
my body to know for sure, man or woman,

and the shock: Was this splitting or growing, adding
or subtracting? I yearned open. Where branch
had been, declivity, cleft.

Is it wholeness I want?

Or fission? Frisson of, its
frequency, its pitch?

Venice

Furtive, that's the version I want.
With eyes averted. Downcast, a little sly.
It's where it's looking, that's
where I want us—
in a harbor where we in our gondola
stare up and up at the enormous
freighters rusting the Adriatic, the ocean
oiled and ropy, scary even,
the way the waters seem higher than
our boat, about to topple onto.
Did I forget to say it's night, we're
seeing by artificial light how thin
flakes of snow are falling from. So easy
to say *the sky,* but that
would be wrong. We could puzzle over
how to say this. Or we could kiss.
Let's kiss, standing up in
scary, its huge hood lowering,
cover of darkness down
which the Crusaders with lances and crosses
high held in a once-upon-a-time still
tarnishing, still audible version
of a version of a version.
There's a vertigo to history different
from the vertigo of sex.
The children sold into slavery, into brothels.
The sores. The futility of crying and the futility
of stories that gradually wash up
on other shores. To what purpose all this

telling, version by version
deteriorating like silk, the patterns
no longer recognizable: ripple by ripple, the lush
lappings as if certain words, *pietà*
or *sofferenza,* were enough.
I had wanted to sightsee, to be taken slowly
by gondola, canal by canal, where Byron,
where shadows on stilts or like inverted
bells somberly under the arches
swaying, and Goethe, who stood on the foamy
crescendos and saw the *chiaro*
nell'chiaro and bibelots
of old and charming, the glimmers
well worn where the moon
all its chandeliers and stairways let down
into the sea-black sea. To stand
on the outstretched lip of
what might be called a romantic evening,
though already that version is
starting to bore me. It's not a question
of what's true or not true, it's more
a matter of what I want to hear.
Which is why we are standing in a boat
perilously small and stiffening
our necks to size the hugeness
of prows—barnacle-studded, ironclad, steely
beaked, with involucral bracts, with
scale on scale, a rust of buds.
Yes, that's how I want us, our love
pressed mouth to mouth

with history, and if with a partition,
then something thin
as lingerie.
I don't want us anesthetized, I want
us terrified and tied to it.
I used to think *it* was teeming, alive
with voices, flashings, with
music in which the dark lit candles.
I tried to reach any way
I could, rung by rung
or with sex shouldering me all the way.
Well, now I think otherwise.
More of a wall or impasse, more of—nothing.
Which isn't to say I'm not moved.
What tumbles through is icy and swift
and doesn't stop. I want us pressed
to that when you shove into me.
No candles. Not even darkness.

Golden Bough

as if it were already the broken-off and they the sheer
weight of the possible: or, as if they
were the broken-off and it
the thrust of all that is necessary, the balance

like a bough swinging lightly
in a breeze, a rush of thought making the air tremble
ever so slightly, and the way notes

cluster in a difficult passage, the dotted
sixteenths sugaring off, almost cloying, the ink
crossed and recrossed, written
over, just this hoard

of ciphers, this acrostic with the bass triads: or as if
the theme were a branch and the notes
bees, a hive of cyclamates, the branch—or do I
mean the melody?—swinging back

and forth, it almost creaks like a gate
opening and closing against
the not-yet, the what is still to come, the notes

swarming to that place, weighing heavily
so the branch tips with its bees
in deep drowse, though
busy, the workplace always going on,

and also: but where the *also* is located, whether
it is part of the continuous, its
music, or whether it comes later, initiating
so to speak, a new era,

workers dipping whatever is thought into huge vats, gold-
plating, stirring the possible until
it hums, the buttery, the sorghum—

I would have preferred some salt, some brine,
the brackish even, some unripe to

lick from the stream from the *miele, mela, meglio, melisma*
the way a bear takes it, stings and all
the unkempt gold like a wedding of finches:

Who would dare break it off?

The Grove at Nemi

Then and *after* were no use to me, nor the desire
to make permanent the impermanent.
The significance everything takes on after rain
was no use to me. I'd come back and it
was not there, not the least shining.
Sometimes there came
one with whom talking went on: *How does foam?*
How does play of light? I would watch the lips
plumping up, the mouth
flapping
its wings, eddying the syllables.
It was like looking down
from a great height.
When below clouded, there was under
with its violaceous twilights, there was down
with its thunders and echoes. On one of my walks
there was a bridge. Was it
ambition I lacked? In its raiments
of cobalt and brown, the river
was naked.
Most sublime achievements, I began.
Bedizenments, I said. *Investiture.*
Toward evening, birdcalls
became stranger, wilder.
What does strange? What does wild? Beyond
the lumber camp, a sound
of flowing,
exultant, indefatigible.
Was it sublimity

I craved? Massive trees were piled up, some
stripped of their bark, and the roots
of a tree dangled
from a machine. In the sky, creamy
utterances. Foamings.
Toward evening, a hugeness.
Some of it moving toward me,
but most of it retreating. Into itself.
Into greennesses untitled.
The flowing splintering, breaking
open, strewing itself.
The surface of the flowing, uneven, bumpy.
In places, the vastness
blurring, opaquing the vacillations, the quandaries
where it hesitated over leaves, over
branches bent into the asides, the digressions.
Toward evening—*What does evening?*
What does open?
What does does?

THREE

Erotikon
(a commentary on *Amor and Psyche*)

1

Some things are still going on, even though it's late, it's dark. Gravity, for example, the pull the earth exerts on the moon and the moon on the ocean. Listening to the tides sweep through the darkness (higher over there, a little lower here), I come to a moment when the ocean lets out a sigh like a train pulling into a station. Its doors slide open, but no one climbs aboard the astral glare of ante meridian.

Giddyap, says the ocean, sometimes

I feel the need for something that does not exist. This wanting is like speed entering a tunnel. *Philia,* said Augustine, keeps everything moving from one place to another. *Orexia,* said Aristotle, because he liked the sound of the word. I want depth in what does not exist and inside depth, the sound of water running. It is a process, too, the nonexistent, and further in, like that lattice of veins behind the eye, a seeing. Or, if not a seeing, what silvers glass into seeing. Darkness on one side, light on the other. As if opposites really did exist, *dúm-duh* and *duh-dúm.* Jetting across the longitudes, it is possible, said Aristotle

to discover the place where darkness begins
to be darkness: night stalled
beside the plane like a cold front, its towers

city blocks palliated and sheered off, battleships

and tenebrous bergs of ice

the shadow of a shade, said Aeschylus, the palpable
obscure, said Milton, and several mention
sables, but there aren't enough
words for night. Why is that? There aren't

enough words for the dark. Show me, said Erebus,
darkness penetrable and darkness penile,

the darkness called skyscraper

but surprise, we are passing through, so not solid, the dark-
ness, though palatial; and twilight, behind us now, how
briefly it endured our passage through veils of diaphanous.
What I want, I said, is a darkness not yet limited to twelve
hours or twenty-four. Swarthy, dusky—they don't do it for
me, they wash off like makeup. Bituminous? The tongue is
barely stained. What I want is a darkness that can run lap
after lap, it doesn't give out, it lives on junk food and nerves,
on dives and divas, on tango and

Up, sideways, and beyond—these, said Varro, are the three
motions of the moon. Oooooooo, we said, *hic jacet* with
herbage and tussock, with verdure and clumps of cosmopo-
lite the moon
                    ossuary
                    bone pot

Give us a hollow sound.
                    Marble?

46

                              Not good enough.
Mausoleum?
              Keep going.
                    I tombi?
With fimbriae, with galloons?
                              With ivy, with rigamarole
and cupids cold to the touch.

What a goof you are. A grand slam of sound is what's needed,
with echoes ambulating the curvatures, with arabesques hexa-
chording the anharmonic, as if the plane had tilted and stew-
ardesses with trays of tea and vodka—a slosh of sound in the
grand basins of the ear. Listen,

sometimes I get worked up, I have to look at the moon rising
between huge chiffonny sails and ships rigged like clouds. So
there is a gap in what you are reading, a diapause where I
began to elongate and drifting slowly, broke apart. Between
the *bes* and *ques* of *arabesques* is a scissors of light, a rip down
the word you were just sounding like a theorbo. Hey, would

you do me a favor? Keep reading, but imagine you have
stopped. Can you do that? Keep reading, but imagine you are
looking at the moon. To help you focus, a soprano is singing
as possibility it is dazzling while a bass recapitulates *where I
began to drift*. Oooooooo, we said, the bivalve attention, *l'at-
tention hermaphrodite*. So many genitals to arouse, all those
tabs and keys to press and the sun honeying the saxophone
and clarinets, shining up a brass meander of light down
which the hereat and thereabout

now bare as retreat, as low tide—
yes, let afternoon be its own pavilion, let indigence
surround, the sumptuous disappearances intoned
through loudspeakers, the less and—

instead of slosh and overbrim
I would look through books in search of some *cwm,*
some *psykter,* words for the eye alone, all
sound squeezed out of them, the listening
ablated: Would it be a real wind or a purely
visual wind filling the valves
of the afternoon, a horn
sounding its memorials, its distances

for the eye only? And the afternoon,
would it be a real afternoon? Or open on one side
like a bathhouse, a cabana, and that place where she kisses him,

that place in the story where so many put their mouths,
is it all listened up, sucked back
into the ear, heard to death?

Just as the fairest leopard is made with his spots, and fire maketh
the gold to shine and the straw to smother, something pushes
through, intoning the off-key, streaking its fuschias like a bad lip-
stick smear across the ordinary, all its radios whiffing, porning the
glee in elegy

And shall I come sweet Sex to thee
bound truelovewise?
O take fast hold, said Sex to me,
of the moneybox, and night was our koine
with its bleats and glottic stops
its suctions and seductions.

All night we laved a fierce lallation.

Wake now, my love, I said to Sex.
Be not overly
subtle with periods and semicolons.
O take fast hold of quim and quid.
By morning I was catamount.
Sex was microcephalic.

The way night comes again and again, it could be happening on
a screen. The way the two bop off each other, night and day,
one of them fragmenting. Then the pieces coming together
again. This is a kind of wordlessness. Bubbles out of the mouth
of a fish is another example. The wordlessness a temptation and
a discomfort. And also none of these.

It was around that time that I began to collect. At first, things
that never happened. Then distinctions that seemed out of
control. And also different kinds of steam. Steam rising up out
of a manhole. Or the sibyl sitting over a hole in the ground,
like a potty, breathing in steam. Also dictionaries. I started
with heaps: sand, gravel, grit, stonedust, sweepings. And what
washes up on beaches; corks and pumice, thorns, balls of tar
barnacled, roundabout and wormtube, runnel, the easily bro-
ken. From these I went on to dictionaries

of the erotic. The way a lover would examine his beloved, checking her parts, the saliva on her tongue with its little suds and bubbles. Sputum. Spit.

Or those furrows water wears into stone, the ciphered, the incised: the finger as stylus, the finger reading a language climbed like steps—*clit   clitch   clitoris*—or stilled as murex, as conch.

At specified times I would go over the gaps and lacunae, the pauses ancient as the backs of giant tortoises. I savored the silences as if they were fabrics, the silks and serifs codified, the serrations and suspirations as if a wind blew through the pages, stirring up ripples and minnows of sound

the wings, the pellicules   pennants in the sea

and pop-up dictionaries, the definitions expanding, with windows that opened and doors through which gleaming, yet indefinite

In one dictionary words were in constant motion, changing as I read them, the way skywriting is stretched into an alphabet of clouds some of the dialects roughened by daily use. Or softened, as if the words had been mixed with that silt a spoon stirs up in Turkish coffee. For example, the word *sparrow* in one dialect was pronounced *shparrow,* the sort of bird that takes crumbs from the hands of young lovers and children.

The dictionaries were indifferent to who used them. Or for what purposes. Some made entirely of pictures. And Catullus could get away with a lot because he wrote in Latin. In one story I collected, the writer had made a fetish of darkness. Everything happened in the dark, the characters seeing nothing of one another. But the reader could see them and the darkness. Darkness was the main character. Wings was another character. And Tango. Reading, I could feel how the writer had rolled the darkness between his thumb and forefinger, how he smelled up all its furs and furbelows. Smoked its cigars. I would watch him in his room alone with the darkness, stroking. This was how he got worked up to write. My reading was interposed like an extra heartbeat: an arrhythmia, a tachycardia of listening. This happened on the expressway too, and in malls. It kept fuming through him, the darkness, which he pressed to his mouth like wet panties, like black lipstick.

After he does it with a real girl, he does it with the other one
in the story. Or with both of them together, the one
with wings lying there on the bed.

The girl in the story shines and glares all over his body
like headlights, his wings beating

the glare of her seeing shivering up his body, and his eyes
all gummed with darkness, cocooned

the wings drenched after he comes, matted, the feathers.
That place deep in where Plato said the soul begins, cutting
its teeth on pleasure, the pleasure raw and bloody from the effort.

When they come together, they fragment. First the girl, then
the one with the wings. His feathers as when a bird is shot,
the bird body pulling apart in the air. That's called orgasm.

Or he is up above looking down on her, so far away he thinks she is
tied to a cliff. He's up where the dome is, where the oculus. Or as if
he were a hawk and she the prey. She feels it pull between her legs.
And breaks up in his mouth like shrapnel. Then she comes together
again. And he breaks up.

And the one thinking this in malls, thinking there aren't enough tenses
for all this to happen in, the past and the present fragmenting as they
bop off one another. There aren't enough words for darkness to make
it different each time. Darkness with smell and without smell.
Darkness with tall buildings, the blades rubbing against one another,
getting worked up. The darkness getting bigger, reaching the tops of
skyscrapers and the one driving the expressway or huddled under a
blanket in the plane, the small laptop resting on her knees

2

I will spread darkness, Darkness said, like a doll on
a bare mattress: broken, the hair matted, silk
scarves and the blackness bunched up, its
boobs and bulbous knobs

Go on, said Tango, feeling it enter her voice,
the unripe, the indigestible, what made
her sick in Crivellis of green

Tango is one character. Speed is another, ablaze and

dripping into the disappearances, the ectoplasmic
rushing away of thinking drizzling off into
fissures, chasms where blackness boils up
uncharted, unimpeded.
                    Along the swagger and irresistible
it's happening so fast there is no space
for breath or wingbeat, only
wave after wave culminating in overmantels and
balustrades with open strings

Speed is waiting for the darkness to go too far, to spoil
go rotten, all its sugars and flambeaus—

I will spread darkness, said Darkness.

Go on, said Tango, forgetting to wipe the excess
from her voice, the scrollwork, she is
strapping herself
into the big boy's wings, lacing up the contraption

for language to change around her
all its green prodigious, as if a parrot
squawking into her ear its guavas, its Cassandras of—

Today, said Tango, the sea is squiggles of stomachache
becoming foam, fat waves crescendoing
into an appetite to be eaten
                              and Speed, Sock it
to me, sock it to me, sock it to me.

                        In the soupy
in the drool there are hardnesses
forthrights and aches where the mind
clamps down on the rushing, on the gurge and

confluence, a movie projector running without
film, no images on the screen to happen
in which golds stagger up
columnlike and twisted, with sputter
                              rusty drippings
screwed into the dilapidation—

Unless, said Darkness, a circle is cut
in the darkness through which, with long lookings and oglings,
at the far end a mirror and across it

to and fro, up and down, from side to side, systematically and also capriciously with motions herky-jerky and half-cocked. But the phrases were beginning to stick together like wet leaves, the possible and the impossible, the seeing getting its jaws around, all foam-flecked. There are, said Tango, twenty-seven kinds of seeing. Or did she mean twenty-seven kinds of wings? Wings with fluff and wings without fluff, wings inebriated with flight and wings descended into their sacs, retracted. The mirror positioned in such a way that looking and gawking and peeping, and even pinhole rooms where a single drop of vision was enough, the body suddenly overexposed. Though of course, said Tango, there is also looking with the mouth open, the mouth like a third eye, as if two eyes were not enough and now a third, a fourth, a fifth—an argosy of eyes like the tail of a peacock spread far and wide. Tango wanted eyes all over her body. But especially an eye between her legs, a great Cyclopean eye blinding her with its salivas and dilations. Think of those lenses an optometrist clicks into place, one over the other as his head looms close in the dark. *Is it better this way? Or like this?* Oh yes, like this, like this. Now it's all so clear it hurts. Yes, unbearable, but sharper, with the brightness of Yankee Stadium floodlit, with hoses of light at full force. Yeah, and why not? thinks the one gliding the expressway, gliding the burning rubber, the acrylic and ammonia. Sometimes this happens with oil refineries to the right and oil refineries to the left. Now he reaches to where it's happening: through bridges and tunnels, with the far lane blocked, with

eyes of the mind, with eyes turned inward on stems of
intellect straining back into the brain where a
wick burns round the clock. *Oh, there!*

With stems of intellect stretched taut, with eyes tuned up
until there begins to open, an inside. *Oh, eyes
of no color opening!*

It was I, Love, that sent eyes into the world, Love that
knocked holes in the skull and shoved
the tongue out. In there, something

for which no experience exists. *Oh, polish it! Burnish!*
And yes, something like fingers are rubbing,
massaging. *Keep at it! Rubbing*

makes it visible. A form. Antler grown from the skull, cold
prong of sharpness, spicule, barb. An idea.
Oh, idea sealed off like a tomb!

As if a kiss with long velvet gloves were stalking,
sneaking up on the darkness starting to thaw,
to wake up like a gong. The darkness

gaining consciousness. *Oh, give it to me! The full glare
of that looking!* Shall I call it Psyche,
that looking? Shall I call it

Soul, those eyes—newcut, sharp and ferocious

as shark teeth? Oh, what shall I call it,
the darkness popping open

like a jack-in-the-box? The brain knocking down walls, push-
ing through bone? And the one driving the expressway think-
ing, Who will speak to me of this? Who needs more than any-
thing to speak? It's your tongue I want in my mouth. Your
tongue with its little bubbles, with its slap and tickle. Oh, bub-
bles, liquid buds of love. Not only those that cling pebbly to
the sides of grass under water or *bup, bup, bup* from the
mouths of fish, but also cartoon bubbles inside which lan-
guage blows from the mouths of men and women. Why not
the aside as such a bubble? A place in thinking so elastic, so
stretchy, it becomes a reservoir of air, an oxygen rush, for those
trapped in slow cars of conversation. Or for those mired in
rush-hour traffic, some bubbly to the rescue. Now he lets loose
a big bubble of fantasy with Tango saying, *Bounce me through
the see-through, Baby. I'm all sneezed out.* Clusters of bubbles
floating at the surface like eggs, like sexual swarm, geodesic
domes of pleasure. And he croons back, *Hey Tango, blow me
some slut and sluice.* And Tango, *Some fast and loose?*

Now! says Speed. Now, before anyone cuts into the tender
undersides of darkness. Now, before the lemon is squeezed
and the darkness uncorks, foaming over.

But do not forget, said Tango, looking that is innocent and filled with wonder, the eyes kissing fervently with parted lids. Or did she mean *parted lips?* And was it Tango saying this? Or Wings? All at once she realized this was to be a story about loss in which even the story was lost. For if there was a story, then there was something, and if there was something, then not everything was lost.

Only Speed wanted to go directly to the encryption, scrambling their favorite places, the possible and the impossible, birds and men with wings.

No love is true save that which loves forever, said Wings. At which they all became sad, for Forever towered above them with its evergreen branches.

Under tuition of the shade, said Darkness. But no one was listening anymore. So Forever let down its check boxes and drop-down boxes.

3

Darkness, light, stillness, and movement originate in one another, said Aristotle, and each exists potentially in each. To transform darkness into movement and movement into light, it is necessary to change the proportion of stillness within them.

But, said Speed, if the proportion of gaze is changed, wouldn't the borders shift, wouldn't the interior rise to the surface

Collapsing, said Aristotle, sky onto earth.

And isn't loss only another fetish? Plato asked.

Darkness, light, stillness, and gaze, said Aristotle.

And what is light, said Tango, if not an invitation to look, to
    press
one's face against looking, to rub one's breath
all over seeing, smudging its transparencies, its sheers
and cellophanes?

To see the darkness lifting its skirts. To see the darkness
undressing to deeper and deeper shades, the hiddenness
pleated, folded over on itself, clavichorded and enrinded
into recesses retiring inward—

Was it a mistake to open it? To let it out of its box?
Impossible now to pack it back in, now that it had sopped up
the sounds of their sex.

What the light interrupted and put a stop to was a process,
said Aristotle, not a process that would necessarily
have culminated in or reached a goal, but a process
in which culmination was always felt as a possibility.

Even when, said Plato, that possibility could not have been
irradiated or developed in the imagination—

It was felt, said Wings, as an expansion of the darkness.
As a throbbing. An aroma pulsing, a song beginning,
breath wafted toward my lips.

In this respect, said Aristotle, the light was like death,
putting a stop to process. Process that was moving
and also process that was not moving.

But that might have moved, said Wings. Its moving
fantasized or felt as a back and forth—

To prolong the throbbing, said Plato. To draw out
the shudder, to rev its wings and engines to erotolepsy.
The way light tattoos the skin with butterflies and lions,
with other lives also desiring, birds with beaks agape.
A love feast of shapes and sensations silk-screening—

My desire, said Speed, is for new desires, new appetites
to hunger and surprise me. To desire tomorrow
what I have not desired today.

There are times, said Psyche, when I need to be addressed by
an author, to hear an author's voice, no other will do, assuring
me, explaining my life to me. It is not so much what the author
has to tell me as his tone. It comforts, it sustains and buoys me.
The author's own faith and optimism that all will turn out well.
The pleasure the author takes in relating my misfortunes. Will I
speak of my own life with such joy? Not a trace of bitterness or
regret?

And the one driving the expressway thinking he'd like to dribble her misfortunes all over his lips. He'd like to take her disobedience into his mouth. Where would the story be without her disobedience? Where would any of us be without disobedience? Tango sighed. History could not manage without it. Poetry would have ended long ago. And all those boxes left unopened. Pandora's and the Box of Beauty that Psyche—

Though, said Apuleius, it is a mistake to think of the two boxes as similar. Pandora's was more of a jar, a little house made of clay, with lips—or was that Pandora? My word for the Box of Beauty was *pyxis,* a small box or casket used for drugs—

Which proves, said Speed, that beauty is a drug. The more you get, the more you need. Or, said Tango,

which intoxicates the beholder so that the rest of life is quickly forgotten, but the one

driving the expressway was no longer listening. He was watching Psyche's lips, how they opened and closed when she spoke, the upper lip gently pushing away the lower, then drawing it close again; how her teeth glistened with syrup. What greeting was worthy of that mouth? Ridiculous to imagine her saying *hi* or *hello* or *good morning.*

Sometimes, said Psyche, I want a bitter taste in my mouth. Is this perverse of me? And in my eyes too. To close my eyes on this taste, so I can make it last. The purpose of beauty is to wash a bitter taste from the eyes.

And in that respect, said Darkness, beauty is not so
different from sleep. Not to sleep is to fast, to keep
the eyes from devouring, from gorging on

the darkness, said Wings.

Speak, that I may see thee, said Darkness.

4

If the darkness were turned off, said Darkness, what then?
Would memory be enough to sustain it, to keep it going?

Toward dawn, said Psyche, darkness is only a ghost
of itself.

Some poems can be talked about, but not written, Wings
observed. Others can be written, but not talked about.

Which kind of poem are we in? asked Psyche. But by then
it was too late, they were already

in The Darkness Box, where the viewer explores every fault
and fracture of eclipse, gashes crammed with disappearances,
fissures descending into zero visibility. When you turn on the
light, the darkness is lit up, darkness still unspoiled, vast
tracts uncharted, not yet memorized. And the light like the
whine of a mosquito, like some small seed stuck between
your teeth. How Tango got into The Darkness Box kept

changing. Sometimes she clicked on Stories Left Unfinished, abandoned structures where the smell of darkness was as fresh as if just painted and the windows like lipstick hastily penciled in. Or she clicked on Spiny Black and descended the darkness as if it were a ladder. Down the windpipe, down the hiatus she went, as

clods of pitch black were spewed up, rough surges that threw open their sarcophagi, stony crypts where darkness hung in clusters like fat grapes. In the infrastructures, in the crawl spaces, it was difficult to breathe, the darkness compressed by the weight of centuries, its molecules following a logic neither straight nor curved, neither active nor passive, but Speed

had already rushed on to Places That Smell of Sex, bathhouses where sand stuck to your legs and the darkness littered the floor like wet bathing suits. Tango lingered in the movie house with its plush seats, well worn, and the gilded gargoyles above the balconies. On the screen the enormous faces of a man and woman. *Click me,* the woman's mouth kept saying.

When they entered The Box of Beauty they saw a beautiful girl asleep or unconscious, a young man straddling her, filling every hole in her body with desire. *Will that be all?* a voice kept asking. The sex performing itself on her, knocking holes in her through which feelings seeped. The sex like a perfume spreading the girl's vulnerability. Or the sex was a shiver in the darkness and the girl spooned out, all idea of her un-ideaed, run back to gruel. Was it beauty that had clubbed her into submission? Or sex? If she could get to where the sex was, Tango thought, but already it was moving on. The box needing her only to open it.

In some places the darkness shone forth like new leaves,
as if it were evolving, putting out stems and branches
almost immediately lost to view,

and a lot of it like badly tied packages, the string coming
loose, hardly any of the darkness in mint condition

nothing stable or permanent and from which lustral sprinklings—

Is this how an idea comes to me? Aristotle wanted to know,
imageless at first, then the way a flock of birds
turns in the air, present, then gone, present, then

the darkness dissipating into troughs which beat up again
as huge wings. Some of the wings tearing away—snotty,
    phlegmy.

Even so the stream of darkness streams back, reentering.

In The Erotikon the darkness was blindfolded. Tango watched her
desire fill in on the screen, first the upper part, then the lower
where the tassels were, the fringes. The fringes were called fetishes.
Ornate rhyme is another fetish. Also snowflakes. And the rain in
Japanese prints which reminded Wings of pick-up sticks, though
Tango said it looked like spaghetti. To get her hands on that rain,
to hold it and rub it, that was a fetish. When someone feels com-
pelled to say over and over *truffle, ruffle, eyeful,* is that a fetish?
Wings asked. But Tango had already clicked Puns, and now her
ears felt like birds flying in different directions.

In The Erotikon Speed's desire was everywhere at once, but Tango could only endure short bursts of seeing. Her desire was that unripe, that irritable in its green and torment of, in the full glare of her temerity looking back at her, giving double her money, all its brazens and gongs resounding. To taste it would be foolhardy, to dawdle in its tarts and dangers, and

yeah, he thought, the one driving the expressway, that's the taste he wanted. More, he said, more,

but Tango clicked on Women Who Disobey and from there she went to Author, where a woman's voice kept saying, *The author is always a woman when he's writing*. And a man's voice confessed, *Now I know what it's like to be a woman, to be excited and have it secret. No one can know what passes through me. When I'm writing, I'm visible and invisible. With wings wild beating* or with wings folded tight as a bud and the way a bud opens, that thin line of gold like a crease of light.

It was a disappointment to everyone that Amore, More and Moira all turned out to be the same place, a room with a weeping girl and a voice repeating, *Loss can be a fetish enacted over and over.* It did not help when Plato explained that *moira* was the Greek word for fate. Whatever, said Tango,

and even Wings wasn't listening because he had found a fetish of his own, collecting words that fit one inside the other like boxes. *Ore* inside *core,* he said, and *core* inside *score.* Tango tried to fit *amore* into *more,* but it didn't work. Try it the other way, said Wings. But then she found *emotion,* and they all played with that one for a while.

It was when the Darkness said, Forget expressways at night,
    moving chains of light, the golden links opening
    and closing,

it was when the Darkness said, Forget remembering and water
    of all kinds, trilling water and standing water,
    water clear and

Forget species, genus, order, class, subphylum, and phylum,
    even though they are delicious as cutting apples
    into halves, the halves into quarters,

even though they are sweet as cutting into cutting, exposing
    the black seeds, the fibers tough as guitar
    strings, saliva-fine threads,

it was when the Darkness said, Forget reflections of clouds
    in puddles, puddles that dry up, and the skill and
    cunning of insects, the lust of minerals,

also trees. Forget their parasites and diseases, and don't
    think of streets with houses elegant as
    isosceles triangles

Psyche asked, Is there a form that can get the better of
longing? In the beginning, Story said,

story held everything together, the darkness and the light,
the little pieces that would have slipped away, the slightest

of them lifting on the first breeze, and even the breeze
would have blown away. Story

was an illusion, said Plato, but necessary. Without it,
no one would have remembered the sunsets and great feasts
and the first time they made love would have pulsed in their
bodies inarticulate. Afterward would have preceded before,
similar experiences would have stuck to one another,
intensifying like a box of matches.

I would have gone on touching her golden hair, said Wings,
I would have gone on rubbing and

said Aristotle, an excess of touching, an excess of intensity
tactile and contactual, an excess at once tactile and
tactless—

So, said Light. Is it ever possible to feel ready, ready enough,
completely ready, on-your-mark ready, on-your-toes ready?

Have you noticed, said Tango, when you repeat the same word
over and over, it begins to lose all meaning?

Have you noticed, said Darkness, but already

it seemed as if light were blowing in with the wind.
The rain was illuminated, and each gust hung with droplets
appeared to brighten the branches it tossed and shook. Or

it's as if light were wrung from the air, said Psyche, from the leaves—

Do you mean rung from the air? Tango asked.

But by then there was so much light, it was impossible to hear what anyone was saying.

FOUR

Golden Fleece

Just like that, I decide to translate a poem that has never
been written, a poem that will be literal and free,
haughty and humble, ornate and spare.

As I work on the translation, I begin to feel close
to its author, so close I can sense what
was in earlier drafts. There it is
like wreckage strewn across a beach.

It is difficult to convey in our language the willfulness,
the animal energy of the original. All those snorts,
growls, leaps, and bounds. To ride that
language bare-assed: no saddle.

The rider's fingers digging in, hanging on
for dear life. The rider giddy, terrified.

Sometimes I think of language as the Golden Fleece.
You know, the ram with great wings
that carried two children across an ocean
a long time ago and spoke
with the voice of a man.

A creature made to get from here to there.
A creature coveted, at least its outer trappings, its fleece,
long after it is dead.

In my translation the Golden Fleece is called
English or American, though I might as well have said
Chinese or Portugese. When it speaks, some
hear the voice of a woman, some a man.

As for who is fleeced, who sacrificed?

It might be more correct to say that after a while
a language grows tired of its riders.

They are shaken off, discarded.

The name of the Golden Fleece was Chrysomallus,
which is like saying the name of the language was Language.

But whether in the original *pluck* was a verb,
as in plucking the strings
of an instrument to make a musical sound, as in plucking
bits of wool that stick to hedges, or a noun,

as in the heart or windpipe of a slaughtered animal—
or a figure of speech, as in courage, heart, nerve,

Hold on is what the ram said. *Hold tight.*

NOTES

Bird: A Memoir

Wimble and wight: Bird has been reading Spenser's *The Shep-heardes Calendar* and other Renaissance pastorals and has twigged two words that were archaic even in Spenser's time. *Wimble* means "nimble," and *wight,* "agile," "quick."

Forswonk, forswatt: More Middle English: *forswonk* means "tired out with work"; *forswatt,* "covered with sweat."

Locus amoenus: "The lovely place" in classical poetry, a place for love. *Locus ille locorum* means "the place of places," "the loveliest landscape or grove."

O Tite, tute, tati, tibi, tanta, tyranne, tulisti! One of the many tongue twisters Bird has collected in a commonplace book, *Erotikon.* This one is by Quintus Ennius (239–169 B.C.) and in Bird's free translation, it reads: "Oh, Love, you tyrant, you took so much for yourself!" A literal translation would go: "Oh, Titus Tatius, tyrant, you took so much for yourself!"

Balls of bright paper: A stocking gift Bird received during childhood Christmases. The balls were made by winding a strip of colored crepe paper around and around on itself, then winding around that core crepe of a different color, which in turn formed a larger core around which the next strip of crepe was wound. It took eight or nine long paper strips to make a ball about the size of a baseball. Bird's pleasure came from the expectation that there was something special secreted at the core, but there was nothing hidden there, and the gift vanished once it was opened.

This wide hugey plain: Bird is recalling *A Mirror for Magistrates,* a long Renaissance poem written in seven-line stanzas. The echoed line reads: "The wide waste places and the hugey plain."

Unheimlicher: A German word meaning "unfamiliar," "uncanny," "strange."

Royal rhyme: Bird means rhyme royal, the seven-line stanzaic form Chaucer used in the *The Parliament of Fowls.*

Where it rocks and cradles: Bird is of course recalling Whitman's great poem from *Sea Drift.*

Pekke hem right up: This comes from Chaucer's *The Nun's Priest's Tale* of a cock and a hen. When the cock, Chauntecleer, has a frightening dream, his wife, Pertelote, an authority on medieval dream lore, attributes his nightmare to indigestion and recommends a laxative of worms and herbs growing in the yard where they live: "Peck them up right where they grow and eat them!" is her advice. Bird, however, has misremembered the Middle English line, which is actually: "Pekke hem up right."

Golden Bough: The Feather Palm

Golden Bough: A bough of gold said to grow on a tree sacred to Diana. When the bough was broken off, a new golden bough always grew in its place. In Book 6 of the *Aeneid* the Sibyl of Cumae instructs Aeneas to find the Golden Bough and break it off: Only when he has done so will he be permitted to enter the Underworld.

Feather Palm: One of several Florida palm trees that as part of their propagative cycle put forth a frond made up entirely of golden-yellow flowers. The flower frond, which is four to six feet in length, seems metallic—made of gold—and therefore unnatural when it appears among the tree's customary dark-green fronds.

Autobiography

Tiresias: A blind Theban seer. He had the unique experience of being transformed into a woman and then changed back into a man.

Venice

The children sold into slavery: The Children's Crusade of 1212, a pathetic attempt to use children to recover the Holy Land from the Muslims, ended with the children either sold into slavery by unscrupulous sailors or dead from hunger and disease.

Pietà or sofferenza: *Pietà* is Italian for "pity," "mercy," "compassion"; *sofferenza* is Italian for "suffering," "pain," but also means "endurance."

Chiaro nell'chiaro: In his *Italian Journey,* Goethe comments on Venetian painting: "All was painted chiaro nell'chiaro"—that is, clearly on a clear background.

Golden Bough

Miele, mela, meglio, melisma: Miele means "honey," *melisma,* "grace notes." But really these Italian words were chosen for their sounds rather than for their meanings.

The Grove at Nemi

The grove at Nemi: The wild grove where the Golden Bough was said to grow in a sanctuary sacred to Diana. Located in the Alban Hills, Nemi and its lake, which the ancients called "Diana's Mirror," still exist. But the locale described in this poem is actually northern Vermont, and the river is the Lamoille. Where the Lamoille River approaches the town of Johnson, there is a lumber camp.

Erotikon

Erotikon: A made-up word created by eliding *erotic* and *ikon*. Parts of this commentary on the story of Amor and Psyche are taken from Bird's commonplace book, *Erotikon,* but material is also drawn from other sources, most important, a fictional website that features a work of interactive web art called *The Erotikon.*

Philia, orexia: Philia is a Greek word meaning "love of one's fellow human beings," "social sympathy." *Orexia* is a Greek word meaning "desire," "longing," "appetite." This is one of several instances where *Erotikon* attributes to real people statements they did not in fact make.

Just as the fairest leopard is made with his spots and fire maketh the gold to shine and the straw to smother: A medley made from phrases found in John Lyly's *Euphues.*

Crivellis of green: In many of his paintings, the Italian artist Carlo Crivelli (A.D. 1439–94) gave the skin of the Christ child a strange sickly green hue.

Erotolepsy: A coined word that means "erotic seizure."

Apuleius: Lucius Apuleius was the author of *The Golden Ass,* which includes the story of Amor and Psyche. Though the Latin word Apuleius used for the box of beauty Psyche brings back from the Underworld was indeed *pyxis,* Apuleius says nothing about Pandora's box in *The Golden Ass.*

The Golden Fleece

Golden Fleece: The Golden Fleece was a fabulous winged ram with fleece of spun gold and the power of speech. Sent to Phrixus and Helle to rescue them from a wicked stepmother, it commanded the two children to get on its back and hold tight as it flew over what is now the Hellespont. Helle, the girl, fell off and drowned, but her brother, Phrixus, arrived safely and sacrificed the ram to Zeus. The marvelous golden fleece was preserved and guarded by a dragon until Jason stole it. The name of the Fleece was *Chrysomallus:* in Greek *chrysos* means "gold" and *mallos,* "a lock of wool."

ABOUT THE AUTHOR

Susan Mitchell has won many awards for her poetry, including fellowships from the National Endowment for the Arts, the Guggenheim Foundation, and the Lannan Foundation. Her previous collection of poetry, *Rapture,* won the Kingsley Tufts Poetry Award and was a National Book Award Finalist. Mitchell grew up in New York City and now lives in Boca Raton, where she holds the Mary Blossom Lee Endowed Chair in Creative Writing at Florida Atlantic University. She is also the author of *The Water Inside the Water.*